The Berenstain Bears **Love** Their Neighbors

Written by Jan & Mike Berenstain

The Berenstain Bears and the **Golden Rule**

Do to others what you would have them do to you.

Created by Stan & Jan Berenstain with Mike Berenstain

The Berenstain Bears **Kindness Counts**

written by Jan & Mike Berenstain

The Berenstain Bears **Get Involved**

written by Jan & Mike Berenstain

The Berenstain Bears®

Living Lights™ A Faith Story

Values and Virtues Treasury

8 BOOKS IN 1

written by
Jan & Mike Berenstain

ZONDER**kidz**

The Berenstain Bears **Patience, Please**

By Mike Berenstain

The Berenstain Bears **Honesty Counts**

by Mike Berenstain

The Berenstain Bears **Do the Right Thing**

By Mike Berenstain

The Berenstain Bears **Show Some Respect**

written by Jan & Mike Berenstain

ZONDERKIDZ

The Berenstain Bears Values and Virtues Treasury
Copyright © 2021 by Berenstain Publishing, Inc.
Illustrations © 2021 by Berenstain Publishing, Inc.

Requests for information should be addressed to:
Zonderkidz, 3900 *Sparks Dr. SE, Grand Rapids, Michigan 49546*

Hardcover ISBN 978-0-310-73495-6

The Berenstain Bears® Kindness Counts ISBN: 9780310712572
The Berenstain Bears® The Golden Rule ISBN: 9780310712473
The Berenstain Bears® Show Some Respect ISBN: 9780310720867
The Berenstain Bears® Get Involved ISBN: 9780310720904
The Berenstain Bears® Love Their Neighbors ISBN: 9780310712497
The Berenstain Bears® Patience Please ISBN: 9780310763680
The Berenstain Bears® Do the Right Thing ISBN: 9780310763628
The Berenstain Bears® Honesty Counts ISBN: 9780310763727

Art direction: Diane Mielke

Printed in Malaysia

21 22 23 24 25 /IMG/ 10 9 8 7 6 5 4 3 2 1

Contents

"The King will reply, 'I tell you the truth, whatever you did for one of the least of these brothers of mine, you did for me.'"
—Matthew 25:40

The Berenstain Bears®
Kindness Counts

written by Jan and Mike Berenstain

ZONDERkidz

Living Lights™
A Faith Story

Brother Bear was a bear of many interests. He enjoyed sports such as baseball, soccer, football, and basketball. He liked to draw and paint, and he was interested in science. He had hobbies like collecting stamps and baseball cards, and he enjoyed fishing and playing video games. But the thing he enjoyed most of all was building model airplanes.

He started building models with Papa when he was very young.
At first, they made simple plastic models. But, soon, they were
creating flying models out of lightweight wood and paper. Before
long, Brother could build models all by himself.

He kept building bigger and better models that could fly longer, farther, and higher. On trips to the park with Sister Bear, he always took along his latest model for flight trials. It was a thrill to wind its propeller for the first time, let it go, and watch it fly across the park.

One Saturday afternoon, Brother tried out his latest creation, a big model plane painted bright red called *The Meteor*. He set it down on the grass and wound the propeller. Sister joined some of her friends nearby. One of them was minding her younger brother, Billy. He was playing with a small model plane like the ones Brother had when he was little.

When Billy saw Brother's big new plane, he came over to take a look.

"Wow!" he said. "That's beautiful!"

"Thanks! She's called *The Meteor*. I built her myself," Brother said proudly.

"Wow!" said Billy. "I wish I could build a plane like that."

Brother finished winding the propeller and picked up *The Meteor*. "Can I help you fly it?" asked Billy.

Brother was proud of his models and careful with them too. They took a long time to build and were easy to break. If you didn't launch them just right, they could take a nosedive and crash.

"Well," said Brother doubtfully, "I don't know...," But he remembered how Papa always let him help out when they were building and flying model planes. That's how he learned—by helping Papa.

"Well," said Brother, "okay. You can help me hold it."

"Oh, boy! Thanks!" said Billy.

Brother knelt down and let Billy hold the model with him.

"Now, remember," said Brother, "don't throw it—let it fly out of your hands. Here we go— one, two, three ... *fly!*"

They both let go, and the big red *Meteor* lifted up and away, its propeller whirring.

"YIPEEE!" yelled Billy. "Look at it fly!"

But Brother was worried. *The Meteor* was climbing up too steeply. As they watched, *The Meteor* rose high above the park. It seemed to pause in midair. Its nose suddenly dipped down, and it went into a dive. *The Meteor* hit the ground with a nasty *crunch*!

15

Brother and Billy ran to the wrecked model. Brother sadly picked it up and looked at the damage. Billy's big sister and the others noticed the excitement and came over.

"Oh, no!" said Billy. "Is it my fault? Did I do something wrong? Did I throw it instead of letting it fly like you said?"

Brother shook his head. "Of course not!" he said. "You did fine. This is my fault. I didn't get the balance right. It's tail heavy. That's why it went up too steep, paused, and dove down. That's called 'stalling.'"

"Are you going to fix it?" asked Billy.

"Sure!" laughed Brother. "'Build 'em, fly 'em, crash 'em, fix 'em!' That's my motto."

"Could I help you?" wondered Billy.

"Now, Billy," said his big sister, "you're too young to help."

But Brother remembered how Papa always used to let him help. That was how he learned about model airplanes.

"That's okay," Brother told Billy's big sister. "I don't mind. I could use a little help."

So Billy came along to the Bears' tree house. Mama and Papa were pleased that Brother was being so kind to young Billy.

19

"It's just as the Good Book says," Mama said, "'Blessed are the merciful, for they will be shown mercy.'"

"Yes," agreed Papa, "and it also says in the Bible that a kind person benefits himself."

"What does that mean?" wondered Brother.

"It means that no act of kindness is wasted," said Papa. "Any kindness you do will always come back to you."

Blessed are
the merciful,
for they will
be shown
mercy.
Matthew 5:7

20

Every afternoon that week, Billy helped Brother work on the plane. He didn't know very much, but he learned a lot and he had lots of fun. Brother had fun too. He enjoyed teaching, and he liked having a helper who looked up to him.

The next Saturday, *The Meteor* was ready for another flight. Brother and Billy took it down to the park. Everyone came along to watch. They wound *The Meteor's* propeller, held it up, and let it fly. It lifted away and rose in a long, even curve.

"This looks like a good flight!" said Brother.

The *Meteor* flew on and on across the field. Slowly, it came down, landing clear on the other side of the park in a three-point landing. Brother and Billy ran over. It was in perfect shape.

"Hurray!" yelled Billy, jumping up and down.

Brother began to wind up the propeller for another try, but he noticed a group of older cubs coming into the park. They carried a lot of interesting equipment and wore jackets that said "Bear Country Rocket Club." Brother went over to watch. They were setting up a model rocket. They were going to fire it off and let it come down by parachute. Brother was excited.

"Excuse me," he said to the cub in charge, "do you think I could help you launch the rocket?"

The cub shook his head. "Sorry!" he said. "You're too young. It's too dangerous."

Brother walked away sadly. But he noticed that Billy was staying behind. He was talking to the older cub in charge. The older cub called Brother back.

"My cousin, Billy, tells me you let him help with your model plane," said the older cub. Brother just nodded. The older cub smiled. "That was cool. You seem to know a lot about flying and models. I guess you can help out."

So the rocket club let Brother hold things for them, carry things for them, and squirt a little glue here and there. He learned a lot and he was happy. When it was time to fire off the rocket, they even let Brother push the button.

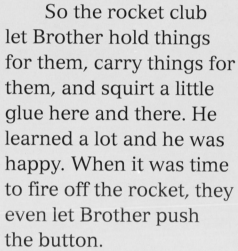

"10, 9, 8, 7, 6, 5, 4, 3, 2, 1 ... *fire!*" said the cub in charge, and Brother pushed the button.

There was a loud *WHOOOSH!*

The rocket shot up, leaving a trail of smoke.

High above the park a yellow parachute popped open, and the rocket drifted back to earth.

They ran over to it. It was all twisted and scorched.

"Are you going to fix it?" asked Brother.

"Sure," laughed the older cub. "'Build 'em, fly 'em, crash 'em, fix 'em!' That's our motto."

"Could I help you?" asked Brother.

The older cub thought it over. "Sure," he said, slapping Brother on the back. "Why not?"

So, because Brother Bear had shown a little kindness to someone younger than himself, he became the youngest member, ever, of the Bear Country Rocket Club.

And was he ever proud!

Do to others what you would have them do to you.

—Matthew 7:12

The Berenstain Bears
and the Golden Rule

Bear Country School

by Jan and Mike Berenstain

37

When Sister Bear received a beautiful golden locket for her birthday, she was surprised and pleased. It was shaped like a heart, and it had her name on it.

"Happy birthday, dear!" said Mama and Papa Bear, giving her a big hug.

Sister tried the locket on and looked at herself in the mirror. "I love it!" she said. "I'm going to wear it all the time."

"It opens up," said Papa. "Look!" He showed her the little golden clasp that you pressed to pop the locket open.

"Neat!" said Sister.

39

She looked inside, expecting to find a little picture or a mirror or something. But all that she could see inside the locket were a few simple words: "Do to others what you would have them do to you."

Sister was puzzled. The words seemed familiar. But she wasn't sure why. "What's this?" she asked.

"It's the golden rule," explained Mama.

"What's that?" Sister wondered.

Do to others
what you
would have them
do to you

Mama's eyes widened. "The golden rule is one of the most important rules there is," she explained. "That's why we have always had it hanging up on the wall of our living room." She pointed to the framed sampler above their mantelpiece.

Sister gazed up at it in amazement. She had seen that sampler every day of her life. No wonder the words seemed familiar! "Oh," she said, a little embarrassed. "I never really thought about what it said before. What does it mean?"

"The golden rule," Papa explained, "tells you to treat other people the way you want to be treated yourself."

"Why is it inside my locket?" she wondered.

"It's a *golden* rule inside a *golden* locket for a little *golden* princess!" said Papa, giving her a big kiss.

"It's called the golden rule," explained Mama, patiently, "because it's precious, just like gold. But it's not about the gold you wear around your neck or on your finger." She held out her wedding ring. "It's about the golden treasure we keep inside our own hearts. The heart shape of the locket is meant to remind you of that."

Sister thought it over. She didn't really get it. But that was okay. She loved the new locket anyway.

The next day before school, Sister showed off her new treasure to her friends Lizzy, Millie, Anna, and Linda. They oohed and ahhed over it in a very satisfying way. "What's all the fuss about?" asked a voice.

44

It was Queenie McBear and her gang. Queenie was older than Sister and a little snooty. When Queenie first came to the neighborhood, she and Sister did not get along at all. Queenie made fun of her and got Sister's friends to join in. That was Sister's first experience with an in-crowd—a group that makes itself feel big by making others feel small.

"Oh, hi Queenie," said Sister. "I was just showing the kids my new locket."

Over the years, Sister learned to get along with Queenie. But they never were the best of friends.

"Let's see!" said Queenie.

She looked the locket over. She was not impressed. She herself wore big hoop earrings and lots of beads and chains.

"Cute," was all she said as she walked away with her friends.

Queenie still had her own in-crowd. They were a group of the older girls who liked hanging out together and acting cool. Mostly, they spent their time painting their nails and giggling about boys.

That was okay with Sister. She had her own group of friends to hang out with. But it never occurred to her that this might be any kind of problem until the new girl came to school.

Her name was Suzy MacGrizzie. It seemed like a funny sort of name. For one thing, it had a lot of Zs in it. The new girl herself seemed a little funny too. Her clothes weren't exactly cool, and she wore her hair up in pigtails, which was definitely not the standard Bear Country School style. Besides, she had thick glasses and braces—not the cool kind with lots of different colors like Millie wore—just plain old braces.

On her first day, of course, the new girl didn't know anyone at all. At recess, Sister noticed her standing off by herself in a corner of the playground. She looked sort of sad and lonely. Sister was thinking about going over and introducing herself when Lizzy and Anna came up.

"Hiya, Sister!" said Lizzy. "We're getting together a game of hopscotch. Millie and Linda are over there. Come on!"

Sister began to follow them. But she paused and glanced back to where the new girl was standing all by herself. The new girl looked lonelier than ever.

"Wait a minute," said Sister. "What about that new girl—that what's-her-name—the one over there? Maybe we should invite her to join in. She looks pretty lost and lonely."

The other girls were surprised.

"Suzy Whoozy-face?" said Lizzy, doubtfully.

"She has weird clothes," said Anna.

"And those corny pigtails," said Lizzy.

"Not to mention those clunky glasses and braces," added Anna.

"Well," said Sister, discouraged, "I just thought …"

"Oh, don't worry about old Suzy MacWhoozy!" said Lizzy, taking Sister's arm. "She'll be fine. She'll find some other cubs to play with—cubs more her type. Come on!"

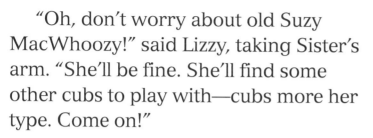

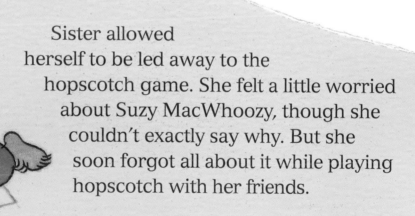

Sister allowed herself to be led away to the hopscotch game. She felt a little worried about Suzy MacWhoozy, though she couldn't exactly say why. But she soon forgot all about it while playing hopscotch with her friends.

Later, when school let out, Sister got in line for her school bus. She noticed that the new girl was standing right in front of her. She was going to say hi, but then Lizzy came up behind her, and they started to talk. They went on talking as they got on the bus.

Suzy MacGrizzie sat right behind them. Sister and Lizzy went right on talking together. Sister played with her new locket as she talked, twirling it around and around in the air.

When the bus came to her stop, Sister gathered up her things to get off. But she felt a soft tug at her arm. It was Suzy MacGrizzie. She was holding something out to Sister.

55

"Here," she said shyly. "You dropped this." It was Sister's new locket!

"Gee," said Sister. "Thanks!" It was all she could think of to say.

Sister climbed off the bus and watched as it pulled away. She could see Suzy looking back at her from the window. Sister hung her locket back around her neck. What if Suzy hadn't noticed her drop it? It might have been gone for good.

Mama was waiting for Sister as she climbed the front steps. "How was school today, dear?" asked Mama.

"Oh, okay, I guess," sighed Sister, dumping her schoolbag on the armchair in the living room. She glanced up at the framed sampler of the golden rule over the mantel.

Somehow, the golden locket hanging around her neck felt heavier than before.

That evening at dinner, Sister was unusually thoughtful. She picked at her lima beans and stared off into space.

"A penny for your thoughts," said Papa as he fed Honey Bear.

"Huh?" said Sister, looking up. "Oh, I was just thinking about that golden rule inside my locket," she explained. "I don't really get it. What's it supposed to mean?"

"Well," began Mama. "Let me give you an example. Do you remember that trouble you had when Queenie first moved to town?"

Sister perked up and paid attention. She remembered it all too well.

"Do you remember how Queenie started an in-crowd but kept you out and made fun of your clothes and hair bow?" Mama asked. "Do you remember how badly you felt?"

Boy, did she ever! Sister started to feel hurt just thinking about it. Her lower lip began to quiver, and a tear came to her eye.

"All the golden rule is saying," Papa continued, "is that you shouldn't turn around and do that same sort of thing to someone else."

He paused to scrape some mashed potatoes off Honey's chin. "You should always treat other people the way you would like to be treated yourself."

"But I would never do anything like that!" said Sister. "Besides, I don't have an in-crowd."

"Oh no?" said Brother, who had been taking all this in. "What about Lizzy and Anna and Millie and Linda? You play with them all the time. But I never see you asking anyone else to join in!"

"That's different!" protested Sister, angrily. "I'm just playing with my friends! We're not trying to keep anybody out!"

"Of course not, dear!" soothed Mama. "I'm sure you and your friends would never dream of keeping other cubs out of your group."

Sister Bear grew very quiet. Now that she thought it over, she wasn't quite so sure—not so sure at all!

The next day at recess, as soon as Sister came outside, she looked around the playground for Suzy MacGrizzie. She soon spotted her, sitting off by herself under the big oak tree at the edge of the schoolyard and reading a book.

63

Sister marched right up to her.
"Hello, Suzy!" she said brightly.

Suzy looked up in surprise.
"Hello," she said shyly.

"I'm Sister Bear, and my
friends and I are going to play
some hopscotch," Sister told her.
"Would you like to join us?"

Suzy's face lit up. "Oh, I'd love
to!" she said with a big bracey grin.
"I love hopscotch!"

"Terrific!" said Sister. "Do you want to see my locket?"

"Sure!" said Suzy.

"Okay," said Sister. "Come on! I'll show it to you … over there."

Sister took off, and Suzy chased her, laughing, across the playground to the hopscotch square where Lizzy, Millie, Anna, and Linda were waiting.

Sister's golden locket gleamed in the sun as she ran.

"Honor your father and your mother ..."
—Exodus 20:12

The Berenstain Bears®

Show Some Respect

written by
Jan and Mike Berenstain

It was a beautiful summer morning and the Bear family was going on a picnic. Mama and Papa packed up the picnic things. Brother, Sister, and Honey were very excited. Grizzly Gramps and Gran were coming too.

"I made a pot of my special wilderness stew for the picnic," said Gran.
"Mmm-mmm!" said Gramps. "Wilderness stew—my favorite!"
"Yuck-o!" muttered Brother. "Wilderness stew—not one of my favorites."

Sister laughed.

"What was that, Brother?" asked Mama.

"Oh, nothing, Mama," said Brother. "Come on, Sis. Let's pick out a good picnic spot."

The family headed down the sunny dirt road
to find the perfect spot for their picnic. Sister and
Brother ran on ahead.

"Wait for us please, cubs," said Mama. But Sister
and Brother paid no attention.

"Hmmm ...," said Mama, none too pleased.

"I remember a good picnic spot right in these trees," said Papa. "We used to come here when I was in school."

"That was about a hundred years ago," said Sister.
"It's pretty run down now. Let's find a better spot."
"Hmmm!" said Papa, none too pleased.

"I know a lovely spot down by that pond," said Mama. "Papa and I came here on our first date."

"That was an awful long time ago," said Brother. "It's full of mosquitoes now. Let's find a better spot."

"Hmmm!" said Mama and Papa, none too pleased.

79

"I recall a time when Gramps and I had a nice picnic on top of Big Bear Hill," said Gran as they went on their way. "There was a lovely view, and ..."

"Now, Gran," interrupted Mama. "We don't want to climb all the way up Big Bear Hill. Let's find a better spot."

"Hmmm!" said Gran, none too pleased.

The Bear family trudged across the countryside. They were getting hungry, hot, and tired.

"I have a good idea for a picnic spot," said Gramps. "How about we all …"

"Now, Gramps," interrupted Papa. "We don't need any help—we know what we're doing."

Gramps stopped short.

"Now, just a doggone minute!" he said. "It seems to me that you folks aren't showing much respect for your elders."

"That's right," agreed Gran. "Brother and Sister are being disrespectful to Mama and Papa."

"And Mama and Papa are being disrespectful to you and me," added Gramps. "You know, us old folks know a thing or two. As the Bible says, 'Age should speak; advanced years should teach wisdom.'"

85

"But, Gramps!" said Papa.

"But me no 'buts,' sonny!" said Gramps. "'A wise son heeds his father's instruction,'" he added, quoting the Bible, again.

"Sonny?" said Brother and Sister. It never occurred to them that Papa was someone's "sonny."

When they thought it over, Brother, Sister, Mama, and Papa realized that Gramps and Gran were right. They were being disrespectful.

"We're sorry!" said Brother and Sister. "We were excited about the picnic and forgot our manners. We'll be sure to show more respect from now on."

"And we're sorry too!" said Mama and Papa. "We know we shouldn't speak to our elders that way."

89

"That's fine," smiled Gran. "All is forgiven. Now come along. Gramps will pick a good picnic-spot for us. He's Bear Country's foremost picnic-spot picker-outer."

"Yes, indeedy," said Gramps. "Besides, if we leave it up to all of you, we might starve!"

"Where are we going, Gramps?" asked Brother and Sister as Gramps led them across the countryside.

"Never fear," said Gramps. "Grizzly Gramps, the picnic-spot picker-outer, is here!"

They marched over hill and dale, through wood and field.
"Now there's the perfect picnic spot!" said Gramps, at last.
"But, Gramps!" said Sister. "That's your own house."

"That's right, young'un," he smiled. "Didn't you ever hear of a backyard picnic?"

Gramps and Papa got the grill fired up and they added honey grilled salmon to Gran's wilderness stew.

"Mmm-mmm!" said Brother and Sister. "Honey grilled salmon—that's our favorite!"

They raised glasses of lemonade to Grizzly Gramps, the eldest member of the family.

"To Grizzly Gramps," said Papa, "Bear Country's best picnic-spot picker-outer!"

"You know," said Gramps, as he dug into a big helping of wilderness stew, "it's about time I got a little respect around here."

"... Always strive to do what is good for each other and for everyone else."
—1 Thessalonians 5:15

The Berenstain Bears

Get Involved

Living Lights™

A Faith Story

written by Jan & Mike Berenstain

Brother and Sister Bear belonged to the Cub Club at the Chapel in the Woods. Preacher Brown was their leader. They did lots of fun things together. They went on picnics,

played baseball

and basketball,

sang in the chorus,
   put on plays, painted
      pictures of Bible stories,

and put up decorations in the chapel at Christmastime.

But the Cub Club was about much more than just doing fun things.

The real purpose of the club was to help others. There was always something that needed to be done around Bear Country. Sometimes it was cleaning up the Beartown playground.

Sometimes it was bringing food to bears who couldn't get out and about.

Sometimes it was even fixing up old houses for folks who couldn't fix them up themselves.

105

Brother and Sister liked to be helpful. It made them feel good deep down inside. Preacher Brown explained that it was always a good thing to help those in need.

"As the Bible says," he told them, "'Whoever is kind to the needy honors God.'"

So the Cub Club went right on helping others all over Bear Country.

Little did they know that very soon their help would be truly needed indeed!

One morning at breakfast, Papa Bear was reading the weather forecast.

"Says here it will rain for the next two days," he said. "Rain, rain, and more rain!"

"Oh, dear," said Mama. "I was planning to do laundry and air it out on the line. It will have to wait."

Brother and Sister didn't pay much attention. A little rain didn't seem to be anything to get very excited about.

On the way to school, Brother and Sister noticed the sky growing very dark.

By the time they reached school, it was starting to drizzle.

Through the morning, it rained harder and harder. It rained so hard that recess was cancelled and they had a study period instead.

"Phooey on rain!" muttered Brother.

"Rain, rain, go away," recited Sister. "Come again some other day."

But the rain paid no attention. It came pouring down harder than ever.

"I think you made it worse," said Brother.

When school let out, the cubs splashed their way home through the puddles. But then they heard a car coming down the road. It was Mama. She was coming to pick them up.

"Thanks, Mama," said the cubs. "We were getting soaked!"

Back home, Papa had a fire going in the fireplace, and Mama spread their wet clothes out to dry. Brother and Sister played with Honey in front of the cozy fire.

"This rain is getting serious," said Papa. "There could be flooding along the river."

"Oh, dear!" said Mama. "That's where Uncle Ned, Aunt Min, and Cousin Fred live. I do hope they don't get flooded out."

Brother and Sister pricked up their ears. What would it mean if Cousin Fred's family got "flooded out"?

At bedtime, Brother and Sister could hear the wind howling and
the rain beating against the windows. It was a little spooky, but
they snuggled down under the covers and soon drifted off to sleep.

They dreamed about
rushing streams

and roaring waterfalls.

It was still raining when they woke up the next morning.

"Wow!" said Brother, pressing against the windowpane. "Look at it coming down!"

As Brother and Sister went downstairs, they heard Papa on the phone.

"Don't worry," he said. "I'll be right over!"

"Over where?" asked Mama.

"That was Preacher Brown," said Papa, getting his coat and hat. "The river is rising fast, and we'll need to get everyone out of their houses down there. We're meeting at the chapel."

"We'll all come with you," said Mama. "There'll be plenty for everyone to do."

Brother and Sister were excited. They had never been part of a rescue mission before.

At the Chapel in the Woods, bears were gathering from all over. Their cars were loaded with shovels and buckets, bundles of blankets, and boxes of food. Grizzly Gus had a load of sandbags in his truck.

Preacher Brown saw Brother, Sister, and some of the other cubs. "I want all you Cub Club members to go along with your dads and help out," he told them. "This is what the Cub Club is all about!"

"Yes, sir!" they said. They were glad to be going. And Brother and Sister especially wanted to make sure Cousin Fred was all right.

The cars drove through the storm, down to the river.

"We're just in time," said Papa. "The water is nearly up to the houses."

An angry river was swirling over its banks and lapping toward the houses.

"Look! There's Cousin Fred!" said Sister.

Cousin Fred, with Uncle Ned and Aunt Min, was leaning out of an upstairs window and waving.

The bears all set to work piling up sandbags and digging ditches to keep the water away from the houses. Brother, Sister, Cousin Fred, and the rest of the Cub Club joined in. They dug and dug and dug until they were cold, wet, and tired.

Then everyone drove back to the chapel to warm up, dry off, and get something to eat.

Preacher Brown's wife, along with Mama and the other moms, had soup and sandwiches ready for all those cold, wet bears. They wrapped them in dry blankets and settled them down in the chapel's pews. Miz McGrizz sat at the organ to give them a little music.

"I'm so glad you're all right!" said Mama to Uncle Ned, Aunt Min, and Cousin Fred, giving them big hugs and kisses.

Preacher Brown got up in the pulpit, opened the Bible, and started to read: "The floodgates of the heavens were opened. And rain fell on the earth ... The waters flooded the earth ..."

Sister noticed a bright light coming through the chapel windows.

"Look!" she said. "The rain is stopping, and the sun is coming out!"

"The rain had stopped falling from the sky," read Preacher Brown.

"And there's a rainbow!"
said Brother.

"I have set my rainbow in the
clouds, ..." Preacher Brown read,
and closed the Bible.

"With God's help, we are all safe and sound," said Preacher Brown. "Thanks to everyone for pitching in and helping out. I particularly want to thank our youngest helpers, the members of the Cub Club."

All the bears clapped for Brother, Sister, Cousin Fred, and the Cub Club. They had been there to help others when their help was truly needed.

"Love your neighbor as yourself."
"And who is my neighbor?"

—Luke 10:27-29

The Berenstain Bears Love Their Neighbors

written by Jan and Mike Berenstain

Living Lights™
A Faith Story

ZONDERkidz

The Bear family was quite proud of their handsome tree house home, and they worked hard to keep it neat and tidy. The trim was freshly painted, the front steps were scrubbed, and the windows were washed. The lawn was mowed, and the flower beds were weeded. Even the leaves of the tree were carefully trimmed and clipped.

135

Most of their neighbors took good care of their homes as well. The Pandas across the street were even bigger neatniks than the Bears. It seemed they were always hard at work sweeping and cleaning.

Farmer Ben's farm just down the road was always in apple-pie order too. Even his chicken coop was as neat as a pin. "A place for everything and everything in its place, that's my motto," said Farmer Ben.

The Bear family had a few neighbors whose houses were positively fancy—like Mayor Honeypot, the bear who rode around Bear Town in his long lavender limousine. His house was three stories tall and built of brick. It had a big brass knocker on the front door and statues of flamingos on the front lawn.

Even more impressive was the mansion of Squire Grizzly, the richest bear in all Bear Country. It stood on a hill surrounded by acres of lawns and gardens. Dozens of servants and gardeners took care of the place.

The Bear family was proud of their neighborhood, and they got along well with all their neighbors.

Except for the Bogg brothers.

The Bogg brothers lived in a run-down old shack not far from the Bear family's tree house—but what a difference! Their roof was caving in, and the whole place leaned to one side. There was junk all over the yard. Chickens, dogs, and cats ran everywhere. A big pig wallowed in the mud out back.

"Those Bogg brothers!" Mama would say whenever she saw them. "They're a disgrace to the neighborhood!"

"Yes," agreed Papa. "They certainly are a problem."

One bright spring morning, the Bear family was working outside, cleaning up and fixing up, when the Bogg brothers came along. They were driving their broken-down old jalopy. It made a terrific clanking racket.

As they drove past the tree house, one of the Bogg brothers spit out of the car. It narrowly missed the Bears' mailbox.

"Really!" said Mama, shocked. "Those Bogg brothers are a disgrace!"

"I agree," said Papa, getting the mail out of the mailbox. "I'm afraid they're not very good neighbors."

Papa looked through the mail and found a big yellow flier rolled up. He opened it and showed it to the rest of the family.

"Oh, boy!" said Sister and Brother. "It's like a big block party! Can we go?"
"It certainly sounds like fun," said Mama. "What do you think, Papa?"
"Everyone in town will be there," said Papa. "We ought to go too."
"Yea!" cried the cubs.

So, on Saturday morning, they all piled into the car. They had a picnic basket and folding chairs. They were looking forward to a day of fun and excitement.

But, as they drove along, the car began to make a funny sound. It started out as a Pocketa-pocketa-pocketa! But it soon developed into a Pocketa-WHEEZE! Pocketa-WHEEZE!

"Oh, dear!" said Mama. "What is that awful sound the car is making?" Just then, the car made a much worse sound—a loud CLUNK! It came to a sudden halt, and the radiator cap blew off. They all climbed out, and Papa opened the hood.

"I guess it's overheated," said Papa, waving at the cloud of steam with his hat.

"Oh, no!" said Sister. "How are we going to get to the Bear Town Festival?"

"Maybe someone will stop and give us a hand," said Papa hopefully. "Look, here comes a car. Let's all wave. Maybe they will stop."

145

It was Mayor and Mrs. Honeypot in their long lavender limousine. They were on their way to the festival too. Their car slowed down, but it didn't stop. The mayor leaned his head out of the window.

"Sorry, we can't stop!" he said. "We're late already. I'm Master of Ceremonies today. I've got to be there on time. I'm sure someone will stop to help you."

And he pulled away with a squeal of tires.

"Hmm!" said Papa. "Maybe someone else will come along."

Soon, another car did come along. It was Squire and Lady Grizzly being driven to the festival in their big black Grizz-Royce. They slowed down too. Lady Grizzly rolled down her window.

"I'm afraid we can't stop," she said. "We don't have time. I am the judge of the flower-arranging contest. We simply must hurry."

And with that, they pulled away.

"Maybe no one is going to stop," said Sister. "Maybe we're never going to get to the festival."

"One of our neighbors is sure to stop and help us," said Mama. "After all, that's what neighbors are for."

"Yeah," said Brother. "But do *they* know that?"

A cloud of dust appeared down the road.

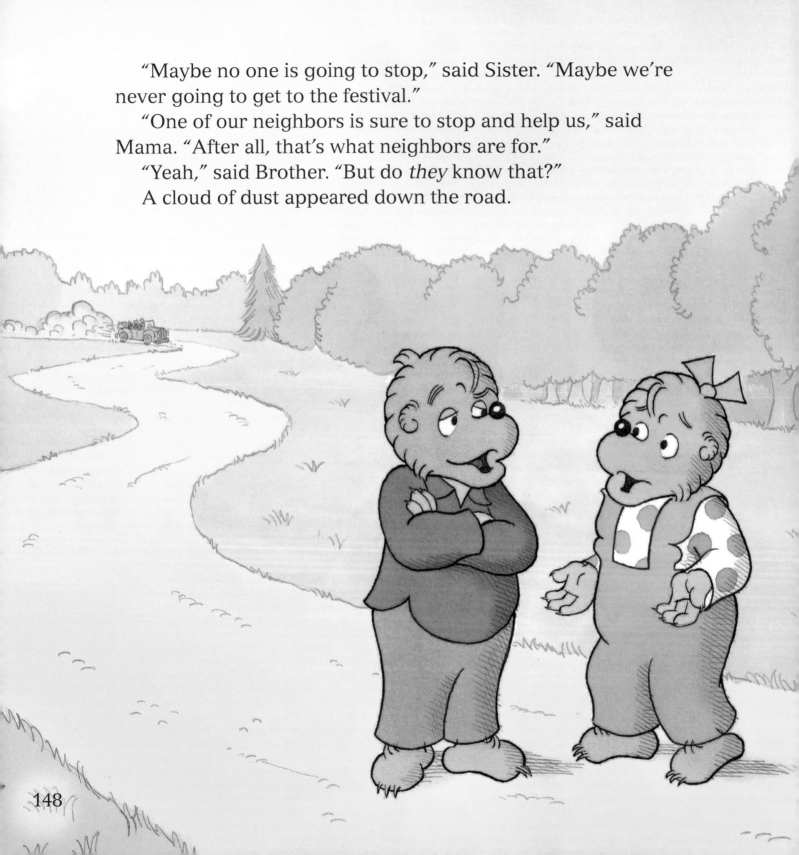

"Here comes someone now!" Sister said eagerly.

The dust cloud drew closer, and they could hear a clackety racket getting louder.

"Uh-oh!" said Papa, shading his eyes and peering down the road. "If that's who I think it is …"

It was!

It was the Bogg brothers.

They came clanking up in their rickety old jalopy and screeched to a halt. First one, then another, then another of the Bogg brothers came climbing out.

"Howdy!" said the first Bogg brother.

"Hello, there," said Papa.

"I'm Lem," said the first Bogg brother. "I can see yer havin' some trouble with your ve-hicle."

"Well, yes, we are," said Papa.

"Maybe we can give you a hand," said Lem.

"That would be very neighborly of you," said Papa.

"Hey, Clem! Hey, Shem!" called Lem. "Git out the rope!"

The other two Bogg brothers rooted around in the back of the jalopy and came up with a length of rope. They hitched it to the back bumper of their car and tied the other end around the front bumper of the Bears' car.

"All aboard!" said Lem. The Bear family climbed hastily back in their car. The Bogg brothers pulled away, towing the Bears' car behind them.

"Where are they taking us?" asked Mama.

Papa shrugged. "At least we're moving!"

Brother and Sister hoped the Bogg brothers weren't taking them down to their old shack. They didn't want to meet that big pig.

They soon pulled into a run-down old filling station. Someone who looked like an older version of the Bogg brothers came out.

153

"Hello, Uncle Zeke," said Lem.

"Hello, Nephew," said Uncle Zeke. "What can I do you fer?"

"These poor folks broke down on the road," said Lem. "You reckon you can fix them up?"

"Let's take a look," said Uncle Zeke.

He looked under the car's hood, banged and clanged around, and came up with a length of burst hose.

"Radee-ator hose," he said. "Busted clean open. I should have another one of them around here somewheres."

Uncle Zeke rummaged around behind the filling station and soon came back with a radiator hose. He banged and clanged under the hood for a few more minutes.

"There," he said, wiping
his hands. "Good as new.
We'll top off the radee-ator,
and you folks can be on
your way."

"Thank you very much!" said Papa, relieved. He
shook hands with Uncle Zeke and the Bogg brothers.

"Thank you!" said Mama, Brother, and Sister. Honey Bear waved. "How much do we owe you?" asked Papa, reaching for his wallet. "Nothin'," said Lem. "This one is on us. After all, we're neighbors."

"That's right," said Mama with a gulp. "We are. In fact, how would you neighbors like to come over to our house for dinner next week?"
Papa, Brother, and Sister all stared at Mama with their mouths open.

"That's right neighborly of you," said Lem. "Don't mind if we do! Shem's cookin' has been getting a bit tiresome—too much possum stew."

"We were on our way to the Bear Town Festival," said Papa. "Would you like to join us?"

"Sure would!" said Lem. "We ain't been to a big shindig since Grandpap's ninetieth birthday party!"

So, the Bear family drove to Bear Town with the Bogg brothers and Uncle Zeke.

They were a little late, but they hadn't missed much …
just Mayor Honeypot's welcoming speech. They all joined in
the games, rides, and contests.

When it was time for the fireworks, the Bogg brothers livened things up with some music of their own.

The next week, the Bogg brothers came over to the Bears'
tree house for dinner. They wore their best clothes and
got all spruced up for the occasion. They even brought a
housewarming gift: a big pot of Shem's special possum stew.
It was delicious!

"A person's wisdom yields patience."

—Proverbs 19:11

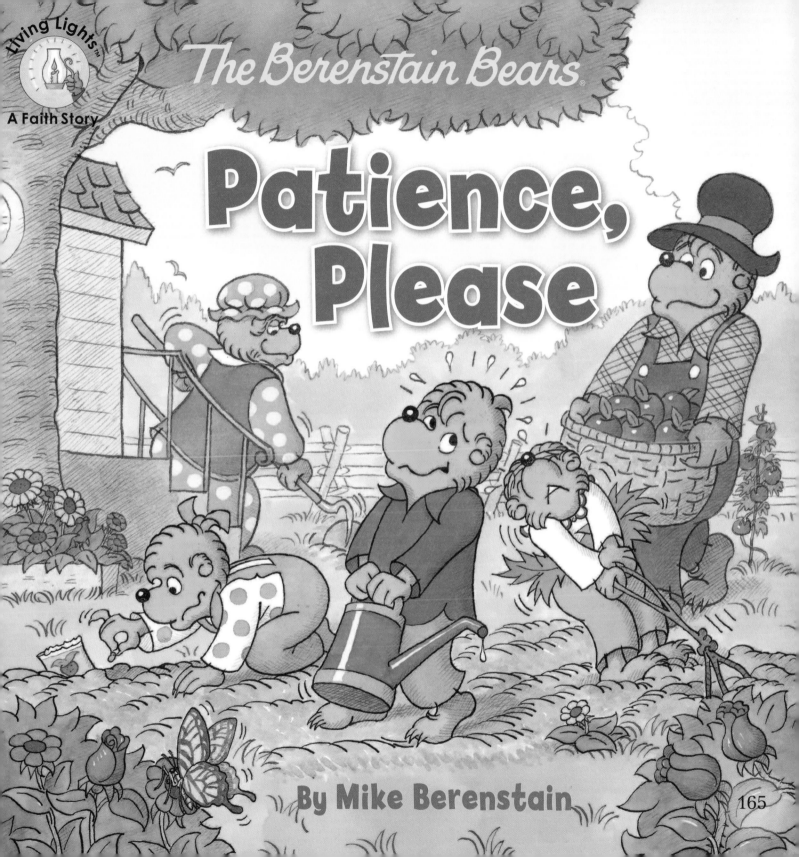

Brother, Sister, and Honey Bear enjoyed helping Mama and Papa in the garden. There was a fine vegetable garden in the backyard as well as beautiful flower beds all around the Bear family's tree house.

167

The cubs helped plant seeds, water, and weed.

They also helped pick the veggies when they were ripe.

One spring morning, as the family worked in the garden, Papa posed a question.

"Cubs," he said, "would you like to have gardens of your very own?"

"You mean we can have our own plots of land?" Brother asked.

"That's right," said Papa.

"And we can grow whatever we want?" added Sister.

"Of course," said Papa, "you'll have to do all the work yourselves. It will teach you self-reliance."

"Yay!" said Honey.

"That's a good idea, Papa," said Mama. "It will help teach the cubs patience too. You have to be very patient when helping things grow."

Papa and Mama guided the cubs in selecting plots of ground for their gardens. The cubs laid them out with stakes and string.

Then the whole family went down to Rufe Grizzly's hardware store to buy seeds.

It was hard to select which vegetables to grow. There were so many different kinds.

Brother chose cucumbers, tomatoes, celery, lettuce, and parsley.

Sister picked carrots, squash, radishes, potatoes, and peas.

174

Honey loved flowers. She stood gazing at the pretty pictures on the seed packages for a long time. Finally, she grabbed a big handful.

The next day, the cubs set to work. It was hot, hard labor. Brother and Sister were very organized.

First, they turned up the soil with shovels and worked in the fertilizer.

Next, they made neat rows and dug small holes to drop the seeds in.

Then, they made signs from the seed packages to mark the end of each row.

Finally, they got out the hose and gave the gardens a good soaking. It did require a lot of patience!

Honey went about things a bit differently. She tore the tops off her flower seed packages and stood in the middle of her plot. She closed her eyes, held her arms out, and spun around and around. The flower seeds flew everywhere.

Brother and Sister were a little startled.
"Honey," said Sister, "I don't think that's going to work.
You need to till the ground before you plant the seeds."

"Pretty flowers!" said Honey, pointing at a picture on one of the empty packages.

"Yes, but ..." began Brother.

180

Honey ran off, chasing a butterfly. Brother and Sister just shrugged.

The next day, Brother and Sister checked their gardens to see if anything was sprouting. But it was too soon.

They went out the next morning too. There was nothing doing. Every day they checked their plots. But nothing seemed to be happening. The cubs grew impatient.

"When is our garden going to sprout?" they asked Mama and Papa.

"You have to be patient," said Mama. "Have faith that what you have planted will grow in God's good time."

183

"Seems to me I remember lines in the Bible about that," said Papa.
"'See how the farmer waits for the precious fruit of the earth, being patient about it, until it receives the early and the late rains. You also, be patient.'"

"That's from the book of James," said Mama.

The cubs sighed, wishing things didn't take so long.

The next day, Brother and Sister wearily trudged out to check on their gardens one more time. All along each row, little green shoots were pushing up.

"Mama! Papa!" they called. "Come look! Our gardens are growing!"

Then they noticed Honey's little plot. Their mouths dropped open.

185

Honey's garden was filled with beautiful flowers. Big ones, little ones, red ones, pink ones, yellow and blue ones. They were gorgeous!

"Well, Honey," said Papa with a chuckle, "God certainly made your garden grow! You've shown us the power of faith and trust along with patience."

"Pretty flowers!" said Honey, happily.

A dove cooed in a nearby tree.

"'Flowers appear on the earth; the season of singing has come, the cooing of doves is heard in our land,'" Mama quoted from the Song of Songs in the Bible.

"I hear the dove, and I see the flowers," said Papa. "Now how about a little singing?" He got down on one knee and sang to Mama.

"My wild bear-ish rose! The fairest flower that grows!"

"Really, Papa!" said Mama, blushing. "What will the cubs think?"

But the cubs giggled in delight.

"Fight the good fight, holding
on to faith and a good conscience."

—1 Timothy 1:18, 19

Living Lights™

A Faith Story

The Berenstain Bears®

Do the Right Thing

By

Mike Berenstain

Bear Town Park was a popular place and a happy place. It was always full of cubs playing on seesaws and slides, batting a ball around, or just hanging out with their friends.

Sister and Brother were headed for the park one lazy Saturday afternoon. They had their baseball bats and gloves, and Sister had a backpack full of her favorite Beary Buddy dolls. She collected them and hoped her friends would be in the park with their dolls too.

At the park, Sister spotted a group of Beary Buddy collectors and made a beeline for them.

"Hey, Sister!" someone called from the baseball field. It was Cousin Fred. "Come join our game. We need a shortstop."

"Yes," agreed Brother. "We need you on our team."

"Sister!" the other players cried. "Sister! Sister!"

Sister liked Beary Buddies. But she liked baseball too. Besides, she was flattered that everyone wanted her to play. She made up her mind. Baseball, it was.

Sister played a fine game that afternoon. She was a talented shortstop and made some terrific plays.

When the game was over, though, her mind turned to thoughts of Beary Buddies.

She looked around for
her collector friends but
they were gone. She could
see them in the distance,
heading for home.

197

Disappointed, Sister turned back to the ballfield. But she noticed something lying under a bush.

Pushing the leaves aside she found … a *Beary Buddy!*

198

It was Chub Cub—a very special doll that was hard to come by. Someone must have lost it—probably Sister's friend, Millie, who had a Chub Cub in her collection. Millie would be upset when she found the doll missing. Sister thought of running after her friends. But they were long gone. She looked at the little Chub Cub doll. It was adorable!

Brother noticed Sister picking up the doll. He wondered what she was up to.

"Sister!" he called. "We need to go home for dinner now."

Sister didn't know what to do about the lost Chub Cub. It probably did belong to Millie. But she wasn't there and Sister had to go home to dinner.

"Oh, well," she told Chub Cub. "I'll think about that tomorrow." She slipped the doll into her backpack with the rest of her Beary Buddies and joined Brother.

After dinner, Sister and Honey played with Beary Buddies in the living room. Brother was reading nearby. The dolls were having a tea party to welcome Chub Cub to their group.

"So nice of you to join us, Chub Cub!" Sister said, pretending to be Foozle Fur, her favorite.

"Thank you so much!" said Honey, pretending to be Chub Cub.

Chub Cub seemed happy in his new home. In fact, Sister was already thinking of him as part of her collection. He fit in so well.

"Chub Cub?" said Brother, looking up. He knew a thing or two about Beary Buddies. "I didn't know you had a Chub Cub. I hear they're hard to find. Everyone wants one. Aren't you the lucky one!"

Hmm, Sister thought. *Was she the lucky one?* She wondered how Millie would feel about that. It made her a little uncomfortable.

"Brother," she said, "can I ask you a question?"

"Sure, Sis," said Brother, reading.

"Suppose someone found something in the park that was very special," said Sister. "Would it be okay to keep it?"

Brother looked up.

He looked at Sister.

He looked at Chub Cub.

"I don't think so," said Brother. "When you find something valuable, like money or jewelry, you're supposed to give it to a lost-and-found or the police or someone like that. Then whoever lost it can get it back."

"Oh," said Sister. She looked at Chub Cub and sighed.

"Brother," said Sister.

"What?" asked Brother, closing his book.

"How do you know what's right or what's wrong if you're not really sure?" she wondered.

"You've got to let your conscience be your guide," said Brother.

"My conscience?" asked Sister. She had heard about 'conscience' but wasn't sure what it was.

"Your conscience is like a small voice inside your head that tells you to do the right thing," Brother explained.

The idea of a small voice inside her head seemed weird to Sister and she looked worried.

"Just pretend you've got a little angel sitting on your shoulder," suggested Brother. "Then, when you're not sure what to do, you can ask the angel and the angel will whisper the answer in your ear."

Sister liked that idea. She imagined an angel in a long yellow nightie sitting on her shoulder. She thought of a question.

"What do you think I should do?" she asked the angel, quietly in her mind.

"You must do the right thing!" the angel answered. "Return Chub Cub to his rightful owner!"

"Okay," said Sister, relieved. "I will. And I'll always let my conscience be my guide."

The next day, Sister returned to the park where she found her friends with their Beary Buddies.

"Did anyone lose a Chub Cub?" she asked, taking it out of her backpack.

"My Chub Cub!" said Millie. "I've been looking for him everywhere!
I was so worried!" She took the doll and hugged it happily.

Then Millie gave Sister a big hug too. "Thank you, Sister!" she cried. "It was so nice of you to bring him back."

That made Sister feel good. She had been worried she would be sad about giving up Chub Cub. But she wasn't sad at all. She was happy. Letting your conscience be your guide turned out to be a pretty good deal.

"Thanks!" Sister said to the imaginary angel on her shoulder.

"No," said Millie, overhearing her, "thank you!"

"You're welcome!" said Sister with a big smile. And the angel on her shoulder smiled back with pride.

"Who may live on your holy mountain? The one whose walk is blameless, who does what is righteous, who speaks truth from their heart."

—Psalm 15:1–2

The Berenstain Bears®

Honesty Counts

by Mike Berenstain

Mama, Papa, Brother, Sister, and Honey were all looking forward
to the Chapel in the Woods' yearly cub campout. Mama checked off
their list of items: sleeping bags, lanterns, picnic basket, tent, matches,
cooking pots, and fishing poles, while Papa packed up the car.

"I can't wait to sleep under the stars," Brother said.

"And we're going to win the annual canoe race down the Rapid River this year, I just know it!" Sister added.

After the cubs got settled, they joined Preacher and Mrs. Brown who were busy sorting life vests and paddles near the river. The annual canoe race was set for later that day.

There would be two canoes in the race. One was paddled by Sister, Brother, Cousin Fred, and Lizzy Bruin—the other by Too-Tall Grizzly and his gang. Soon everyone was gathered around.

"The race will go down the rapids and around the bend in the river to the finish line at the old oak tree," announced Preacher Brown. "We'll meet up there!"

Finally, the time came. The two teams pushed their canoes into the water.

"Ready, get set ... PADDLE!" called Preacher Brown.

The teams paddled as fast as they could. At first, the two canoes were neck-and-neck. Then, Brother and Sister's canoe pulled ahead. They were better paddlers than the Too-Tall gang.

"Look out!" called Lizzy. "We're coming to the rapids!"

White water boiled up ahead of them.

"Stroke! Stroke! Stroke!" called Brother as they shot into the rapids.

They swept past Big Bear Rock.

"Stroke! Stroke! Stroke!" called Lizzy as they curved
around Swirling Whirlpool.

"Stroke! Stroke! Stroke!" called Fred as they bumped down Twenty Steps Falls.

When they reached the bottom, they looked back. The Too-Tall gang was nowhere to be seen.

"I guess they decided not to risk the falls," said Brother.

"Hooray!" cried Sister. "We're going to win!"

"Hooray!" they all cried.

But as the cubs drifted around the bend in the river, they saw an amazing sight. There, tied to the old oak tree that marked the finish line, was a canoe. And there, leaning against the tree, was—*the Too-Tall gang!*

The cubs' mouths hung open.

"How," they gasped, "did you get ahead of us?"

"Nothin' to it!" said Too-Tall with a grin. "We just paddled around one side of Big Bear Rock while you paddled around the other side."

"Yeah!" smirked gang member Skuzz. "You were so busy with your 'Stroke! Stroke! Stroke!' that you never noticed us."

The gang began to dance around pretending to paddle.
"Stroke! Stroke! Stroke!" they chanted.

Just then, Preacher Brown and the other campers came up to see the end of the race.

"So, that's all there was to it, eh, Too-Tall?" said Preacher Brown, folding his arms. "Are you sure you're being completely honest?"

"What do you mean?" asked Too-Tall, nervously.

"It seems to me I remember a shortcut around here ..." said Preacher Brown. He pushed aside a clump of cattails at the water's edge.

"Look!" cried Lizzy. "It's a hidden creek!"

"A shortcut!" said Brother. "Too-Tall never went down the rapids. He just paddled down this hidden creek to win the race!"

"You cheated!" they yelled at the Too-Tall gang. "You were dishonest!"

"Well, I guess we were … *a little!*" admitted Too-Tall.

"Too-Tall," said Preacher Brown, shaking his head, "'An honest witness tells the truth, but a false witness tells lies.'"

"That's Proverbs chapter twelve," said Fred, who liked to memorize things. "And it says, 'The words of the reckless pierce like swords, but the tongue of the wise brings healing.'"

"Whoa!" said Too-Tall, imagining the Bible verses coming alive with swords and tongues. "Awesome!"

"Yes," agreed Preacher Brown. "The blessings of honesty are awesome, indeed!" And with that, Preacher Brown awarded Sister, Brother, Cousin Fred, and Lizzy blue ribbons for winning the race fair and square.